PANDORA
OF ATHENS
399 B.C.

☙ ☙ ☙

THE LIFE AND TIMES

PANDORA OF ATHENS

399 B.C.

⚜   ⚜   ⚜

BY BARRY DENENBERG

Scholastic Inc.   New York

⚓

Library of Congress Cataloging-in-Publication Data

Denenberg, Barry.
Pandora of Athens : 399 B.C. / by Barry Denenberg. — 1st ed.
p. cm. — (Life and times)
Summary: In 399 B.C. in Athens, thirteen-year-old Pandora dreads her
upcoming marriage to a man twice her age, but a chance meeting with the
philosopher Socrates encourages her to question traditional female roles and
to seek her own truth.
ISBN 0-439-64982-X
1. Socrates—Juvenile literature. [1. Socrates—Fiction. 2. Conduct of life—
Fiction. 3. Sex role—Fiction. 4. Philosophers—Fiction. 5. Athens (Greece)—
Fiction. 6. Greece—History—Spartan and Theban Supremacies, 404-362
B.C.—Fiction.] I. Title. II. Life and times (Scholastic)
PZ7.D4135Pan 2004
[Fic]—dc22   2004002500
10   9   8   7   6   5   4   3   2   1   04 05 06 07 08

The display type was set in Athenaeum.
The text type was set in Mrs. Eaves.
Book design by Elizabeth B. Parisi

Printed in the U.S.A.
First edition, October 2004

⚓

ACKNOWLEDGMENTS

The author would like to thank Kerry Blassone,
Amy Griffin, Beth Levine, Liz Usuriello, Terra McEvoy,
and everyone at Scholastic.

CAST OF CHARACTERS

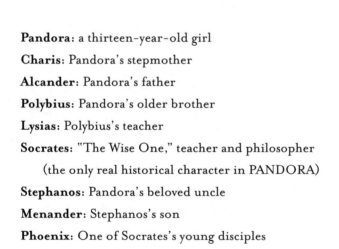

Pandora: a thirteen-year-old girl

Charis: Pandora's stepmother

Alcander: Pandora's father

Polybius: Pandora's older brother

Lysias: Polybius's teacher

Socrates: "The Wise One," teacher and philosopher
(the only real historical character in PANDORA)

Stephanos: Pandora's beloved uncle

Menander: Stephanos's son

Phoenix: One of Socrates's young disciples

A Life Without Love

⚜ ⚜ ⚜

The Wise One told her the story of her name.

"Do you know of the first Pandora?" he asked.

She didn't, this being the very first time she had heard of anyone but her being named Pandora, a fact of which she was, previously, quite proud.

"It all began a long, long time ago, before the earth and the sea were created. Almost at the beginning of time, really, when all was dark and silent. There were only gods back then, and Zeus was the father of all gods.

"Zeus charged Prometheus with the task of creating the first animals and man.

"Zeus did not want man to have fire and hid it from him. But Prometheus wanted to give man something that would distinguish him from the animals. He went up to heaven, where the sun was, lit a torch, and brought fire back down to the earth. Now man could

make weapons to subdue the animals, fashion tools to cultivate the earth, cook his food, and warm himself and his dwellings.

"This treacherous act angered Zeus beyond all description. As punishment, he had Prometheus bound by steel chains to the side of a mountain and commanded an eagle to endlessly tear at his liver.

"And Zeus wasn't finished.

"Man, too, had to be punished and his punishment would be woman.

"He ordered the earth to be mixed with water and the first woman to be formed from the resulting clay. He vowed to make her so lovely to look at she would be irresistible to man.

"He ordered all the gods and goddesses of Mount Olympus to contribute their special gifts and named her Pandora, meaning 'all gifts.'

"From Athena, Pandora received the talent to weave her magnificent garments; Aphrodite, the goddess of love, bestowed upon her the face and form of physical perfection; Apollo gave her the love of music and poetry.

"After she was given a most tempting human voice, the Four Winds breathed life into her.

"Now, Prometheus had a brother named Epimetheus. Prometheus was wise, but his brother was not so wise. Prometheus warned him not to accept any gifts from Zeus no matter how appealing. But Epimetheus, upon seeing the extraordinary Pandora, was seduced by her beauty and charm and foolishly made her his wife.

"Pandora tried hard to enjoy her new, married life, but because of the jar she was unable to. The jar, really a rather large, lidded clay vessel, had always been with her. She couldn't remember a time when it wasn't — as if it were part of her, which, indeed, it was.

"And there was never a time when she wasn't aware that she was not to open it — not ever.

"She would stare at the jar for hours, wondering what was inside. Sometimes it was all she could think about. No matter how pleasant and peaceful her day, the jar was never far from Pandora's mind.

"Her husband periodically reminded her that the gods had warned that the jar must never be opened.

"But it was too much for Pandora.

"Early one morning, while Epimetheus was away, she lifted the lid ever so slightly and was immediately thrown to the ground by the terrific force spiraling up from the opening. An ill wind escaped from the jar and turned into a black cloud that funneled out through the window and dispersed into the world.

"That ill wind contained all the blessings and curses of mortality."

⚹

Just then the Wise One's followers rushed in, breathlessly admonishing their sometimes forgetful master that he was late for an important appointment. The Wise One was ushered out, with no time to bid Pandora farewell.

The story left Pandora pleased but saddened.

Pleased to be named after the first woman, and a most beautiful and beguiling one at that. But saddened that her namesake was the bearer of all the woes of mortality.

She thought about this for quite some time, finally concluding that the life of man before Pandora, before woman, that is, must have been, well, boring.

Boring because without pain there could be no joy. Without lies no truth. Without suffering no relief. And, most important, without passion no love. Without woman there would be no love.

And Pandora could not imagine a life without love.

PART
ONE

A WAY OUT

Pandora tried to learn what was expected
of proper Athenian girls: spinning thread and weav-
ing wool and flax; kneading dough and baking bread;
shaking out blankets; making up the fires; locking up
the silver; bolting the door separating the upstairs
women's quarters from the downstairs men's quarters (otherwise, she was warned, the slaves would steal
and do unspeakable things to one another); and balancing a clay vessel on her head on the way to the
Fountain House.

She didn't actually mind doing any of those
things. In fact, going to the Fountain House was, besides going to her friend Apollonia's house to borrow
or return lamp oil, the highlight of Pandora's day.

What she did mind was being confined to the

house all day. In Athens, respectable girls — her stepmother Charis reminded her more than once — remained at home. Once, when she was ten, she had stood on the roof, just to see what was going on. Alcander, her father, told her that was forbidden. That same year, she asked why it was all right for the slave girls her age to go on errands but not her. "To be protected from the prying eyes of strangers" was the unsatisfying answer from her father.

"What is outside the house is men's business," her father reminded her, his lisp ever more annoying than usual. She had heard him often enough on the subject.

"A woman who thinks is a terrible thing."

"The proper role of women is to get along with men."

"Teaching a woman is like giving more venom to a snake."

Only yesterday, he returned from the Theater of Dionysus, imitating the actor who had delivered his favorite line:

"Silence is a woman's glory."

Alcander fell asleep, collapsing on the terrace to take advantage of the summer night's breeze. Shortly thereafter, he had gone to one of his after-theater banquets. He was blissfully unaware that his daughter had wanted to see the play — any play. The idea of watching actors perform a story while seated in the audience on the south side of the Acropolis, fascinated Pandora to no end. Had Alcander known that it angered her that only men could attend the theater, her father would have been speechless — a rare state for him.

When it came to women, her father believed in the three *s*'s: silence, submission, and suffocation.

When Pandora had been younger — protected by the innocence of youth — things like this didn't bother her. Or at least she didn't remember that they had. But now she was thirteen, no longer a child, and they did. More and more with each passing day.

She disliked spending the entire day with the female slaves, walking around in her nightdress. It was boring and Pandora hated to be bored.

It wasn't only being able to see the play. She wanted to feel the sun on her face, to see the world outside her door.

She wondered and was curious.

Thousands of questions were bubbling up inside her head, threatening to come to a boil and spill over.

Her life seemed empty, her future desolate.

She longed for a way out.

Fashionable Ladies

⁂ ⁂ ⁂

Pandora thanked the gods that her father didn't, like her friend Apollonia's father, insist that she cover her face with her cloak when she went to the Fountain House. Balancing the clay vessel on her head was quite enough without having to worry about hiding her features from the gaze of strangers.

Pandora looked forward to her daily trips to the Fountain House. It was her only chance to talk with other girls and to look around. To see things.

Pandora wished they weren't so rich. If they were poor, they wouldn't have so many slaves, and maybe then she would have to work outside the house, a thought that absolutely delighted her.

She fantasized about what it would be like working as a washerwoman or a dressmaker. Or even better, a flower seller in the agora.

She remembered vividly the first and only time she went to the agora. It was two years ago, and her father had to take her with him for some reason. Pandora could tell immediately that he was annoyed, and she could guess why. Because of her he wouldn't be able to spend as much time as he liked — all day, that is — chatting away at the barbershop, the baths, and the gymnasium.

They ate quickly — some bread and a handful of figs from the tree that grew just below Pandora's bedroom window.

First they went through the narrow, twisted, and dusty streets to the Ceramicus, the Potters' Quarter. They saw the potters and their kilns. Her father perused the pots, searching the stacks for ones painted with pictures of the gods. Those were his favorites.

Pandora enjoyed watching the potter as he slowly turned his wheel and shaped the pot in his hands, transforming a lump of clay into a beautiful vessel. After he carefully set it in the sun to dry, he painted black figures on the red-dyed clay of one of the pots that had already been fired in the kiln.

After that they went to the central marketplace. The agora was already crowded, and everyone was talking loudly and simultaneously. Pandora couldn't believe something like this actually existed, anywhere, let alone right here in Athens.

There were endless rows of stalls manned by craftsmen and shopkeepers selling goods that came from all over the Greek world: vegetables, cheeses, wines and olive oil, cosmetics and perfumes, flowers, pigs, lamps, old clothes, hardware, and books. Everything was laid out under the awnings and large umbrellas.

There seemed to be an argument of some sort going on at every stall. One man said he was being overcharged, another claimed he had been shortchanged, and still another was complaining about the quality of something he had bought previously.

The fish stalls were the most crowded. Her father looked over the incredible variety of fresh seafood: bass, mackerel, tuna, squid, octopus, sardines, and anchovies. Finally, after much haggling, he settled on the largest eels he could find, the ones from Lake Copais.

The prettiest stall was the one with the violets made into garlands and the gorgeous display of dark blue hyacinths. Pandora adored hyacinths and wished they could bring some home to her stepmother. But by then her father was busy greeting everyone he knew and getting something to eat from the sausage vendor.

While he talked, Pandora watched the drama taking place at the cobbler's. His shoe shop was nearly as crowded as the fish market, only it was a decidedly different crowd. All his customers were fashionable ladies, and they were all demanding his attention at the same time, resulting in a somewhat frenzied atmosphere.

Pandora had never seen women who didn't wear the same drab wool and linen garments that she did. These women wore saffron-dyed gauzy chitons that swirled about them as they walked, although walk was hardly the word for the way they moved. Prance would be more like it, like highly charged chariot horses awaiting the start of the race. Pandora couldn't imagine how they walked like that, considering the platform shoes they wore to make them look even taller and more elegant than they already were.

And their complexions — they were so white, with just a touch of rouge on either cheek. Each one carried a parasol to protect her from the harsh rays of the sun.

The cobbler was bouncing from one to another, trying to satisfy them all, while his assistants scurried around, randomly picking up a discarded pair of shoes from time to time but accomplishing little else.

Pandora was dazzled by the incredible variety of styles and colors that the cobbler presented to these fashionable ladies. There were canary yellow espadrilles, scarlet slippers, blue high-button boots, and sandals and pumps in all sizes, shapes, and hues.

The fashionable ladies bantered and joked with the cobbler as though they were his lifelong friends, although it was quite obvious that they weren't. They warned him not to make his prices too high or else they would leave.

Pandora was stunned to hear that a pair of boots that one of the ladies was buying cost 100 drachmas. She wanted to ask her father if this was possible but suddenly was interrupted. A cloak snatcher had been caught, and the crowd was in a frenzy.

As Pandora and her father left, they passed the slave market. Pandora saw a small, black slave boy who was crouching down. His knees were drawn up to his chin, and he pulled his legs close to him with his arms, resting his weary head on top of his knees, not looking up.

Pandora couldn't tell if he was trying not to be noticed or if he was trying to disappear.

Pandora returned home reluctantly. She couldn't remember ever having such a good time — ever seeing so much, smelling so much, or hearing so much.

When Polybius, her older brother, came home, she asked him about the fashionable ladies she saw in the shoe stall. "Where did they come from?" she asked, assuming that they couldn't possibly be from Athens.

Her brother, who had regrettably begun talking like her father lately, said that Pandora "shouldn't concern herself with those kinds of women," which she didn't understand. She didn't want to "concern herself" with them, whatever that meant. She just wanted to be able to walk like them and talk like them.

White Was Black

❧   ❧   ❧

Pandora didn't approve of envy, but she had to admit that she was envious of her brother's freedom. Polybius came and went as he pleased, especially now that he was seventeen.

She watched him when he eagerly headed off to his rhetoric lessons, wishing she, too, had someplace she was eager to go to.

Pandora had to admit that her brother's course of study was quite rigorous: grammar, literature, history, politics, geometry, physics — all in addition to rhetoric.

Lysias, his teacher, had already taught Polybius to write — something Pandora longed to learn, as she longed to read. He had painstakingly traced the letters his teacher drew faintly on the wax-coated tablet until he could do it quite well all by himself. Polybius could not only write with a stylus but could also write on papyrus with a reed that he trimmed and dipped in the ink he made.

His progress was remarkable — when he first began his rhetoric lessons, he was a babbling boy of fifteen, hardly able to string two coherent sentences together. Now, only two years later, he was already delivering persuasive speeches on a variety of subjects, none of which interested Pandora. Polybius was gaining a reputation around Athens as a fine public speaker — someone to keep an eye on.

When he was younger, he liked to practice defending his friends against one another, not caring whose side he took first — then switching to show how he could win no matter which side he took.

Lately, Polybius spent his time down at the seashore, making his voice heard over the crashing surf. He composed practice speeches, which he gave to his pet monkey. Someday, he boasted, he would be speaking in front of the Assembly when they met on the Pnyx, the hill near the Acropolis, and in the law courts.

Alcander had taught Polybius to read aloud when he was quite young. By the time he was eight, he could already recite all of Homer — the *Iliad* and the *Odyssey* — by heart, astonishing everyone around him.

Polybius was all Pandora's father ever cared about; she had always known that.

She was impressed by how skillful her brother had become, but skillful at what? What he was learning sounded more like the art of twisting the truth rather than arriving at the truth.

She heard him and his new friends — for now he only associated with boys who were taught by Lysias — laugh at the distinction between truth and lies. To them there was no difference. They bragged about their ability to debate successfully no matter what side of an issue they took. They were proud they could argue that white was black and black, white.

Alcander told everyone he knew, and some he didn't, how proud he was that Lysias had consented to take Polybius on as a pupil. According to Alcander — who was known to inflate the truth from time to time, especially if it made him look good — Lysias was quite particular about his students. He only took the qualified sons of the *very best* families in Athens, which apparently they were.

Being considered one of the very best families in Athens was very important to Pandora's father.

He also liked to tell them, whether they wanted to hear it or not, about the substantial fees that Lysias demanded. Ten minas, which many found hard to believe. Alcander was delighted when he saw the look of astonishment that came across their faces. He never considered that some were astonished because he was so superficial and transparent.

Lysias, he went on, was the most learned man in Greece, and he was going to pass all of that knowledge on to Polybius. His expertise in teaching rhetoric — "the art of persuasive public speaking," he explained condescendingly — was unsurpassed. Lysias had guaranteed him that when he was through with his son, the sky would be the limit.

Boasting was one of Alcander's favorite pastimes. It was fast becoming one of Pandora's brother's, too.

Strange and Mysterious

Her brother's mind wasn't the only thing that was developing. Right before Pandora's eyes he had been transformed from a scrawny teenager into a muscular man, thanks to the countless hours he spent at the gymnasium.

Her own body was changing, as well. It was happening so fast at times she was breathless. Each morning, or so it seemed, there was something new. Some of it pleasing, some of it disturbing, all of it strange and mysterious.

She was grateful that she could talk to her stepmother, who was much younger than her father and only ten years older than Pandora.

Charis came to Athens only three months after Pandora's mother had died. Even though Pandora was only five she could see that her new mother was different. Polybius said that was because she was from Sparta, and according to him, Spartans were not like regular people. They didn't even speak the same dialect as Athenians. Polybius hated Spartans, like nearly everyone else in Athens except their forgiving uncle Stephanos. He never understood why his father couldn't have married someone from home.

As far as Polybius was concerned, it was about money. Charis came from a rich family — they had made a fortune breeding racehorses. And she brought with her a very large dowry: 12,000 drachmas, according to her brother to whom such calculations were immensely important.

Polybius may have been concerned with why his father married Charis, but for Pandora the mystery went the other way.

Pandora loved to hear her stepmother tell stories about what it was like to grow up in Sparta. The fact that she told these stories only to Pandora was what Pandora liked best of all.

Pandora adored Charis. She was the most beautiful woman she had ever seen. She had a creamy complexion; a long, lean body with muscular legs; and round breasts that were not too large like many

of the slave girls' breasts. She exercised every morning — bringing her heels up to her buttocks 500
times — to make sure she stayed in shape.

Pandora hoped that someday she would be as
pretty as her. She was already almost as tall.

As she grew, Pandora took instructions from her
stepmother on ways to take care of herself: how to use
a razor on unwanted hair, and then Charis discreetly
left her woolen rags to use when the time came.

Her stepmother showed her how to fashion her
long, thick, auburn hair into an elaborate but elegant hairstyle with a twist encircling the back and a
wavy section in front or just a single, simple braid
going straight down her back. Her hair was, Pandora
thought, her best feature (her hazel eyes were a close
second). She combed it carefully every day, arranged
it neatly at night, and fixed it prettily in the morning even though there was never anyone around to
appreciate it.

Her precious mirror was her first gift from her
stepmother, and Pandora made good use of it. She
worried that her neck was too short and thought
that stretching it might help. Her stepmother said it
probably wouldn't hurt as long as she didn't stretch
it so far that her head popped off.

Pandora was startled to hear how different Sparta was from Athens. It sounded not like another city but another world.

Unlike Athens, where girls ate small portions of plain food and were not allowed to drink wine, Spartan girls ate as much as the boys. Spartans believed that girls should have plenty of proper nourishment so that their bodies would be prepared for pregnancy and childbirth. They even washed newborn babies in wine to test their strength and improve their health and didn't even swaddle them.

And girls exercised as much as boys for the same reason. Pandora's stepmother competed against boys in the long jump and knew how to throw a discus and a javelin. Sometimes they exercised in the nude.

One time she wrestled against a girl who had coated herself with so much olive oil that it made Charis sick and she lost.

The life of Spartan boys was even more fascinating. When they were seven they were taken from their mothers and placed in military barracks with other boys. There they ate, slept, and lived together while learning to be fierce, professional soldiers.

Pandora liked hearing about how Spartans

decided on whom they would marry. "Marriage by capture," it was called. All the girls and boys in a particular area were locked up together in a dark room and whoever caught you, that's whom you married.

Pandora asked Charis what she missed most of all about Sparta. Her stepmother said she missed riding her father's racehorses and wearing her short, thigh-high skirts, which she could never wear in Athens, not even around the house. Pandora wanted to ask her stepmother if she were glad her marriage to Alcander had been arranged for her but was too timid.

Once, while working on her loom, the shuttle rattling as they talked, Charis asked Pandora if she had been frightened when she found out she was getting a new stepmother, especially one she had never met.

Pandora told her that the slaves had talked about how wicked stepmothers were. That had scared her, but Pandora said that as soon as she saw her new mother's face, she knew she had nothing to fear.

Discovery and Delight

Discovery and Delight

❖ ❖ ❖

Then one day Pandora's life changed utterly and forever.

She was walking down the hill to the Fountain House, thinking how much easier it would be if she could walk up the hill so that she would be transporting the full vessel down. And she was wondering why it was that only women knew how to balance water vessels on their heads, thinking that maybe men just didn't want to know how so they would never have to do it.

Despite her complaints, Pandora was still glad they didn't have a well in their courtyard so she could get out of the house once a day.

Even when she was only halfway down the hill she could see that there was a large crowd gathered at the Fountain House: a most unusual occurrence.

When she got closer, Pandora saw Apollonia and asked her friend what all the fuss was about. Apollonia could only offer that someone was talking to someone about something, although she didn't know who or what.

Pandora knew that a crowd didn't form at the Fountain House every time two people had a discussion. Obviously, she thought, something very important was happening, but she wasn't going to find out from Apollonia.

Pandora decided to worm her way through the crowd so she could get a better view of what everyone was looking at.

After depositing the water vessel on the ground at the fringes of the crowd, she began elbowing her way to the center. When she broke through the front ranks, she saw that the crowd had formed a semicircle around two men: one, an older man sitting on a large rock and another, younger man who was standing and doing the talking.

The man sitting on the rock was old — at least seventy, older even than Pandora's father. He was ragged, dirty, barefoot, and quite ugly. He had a white beard, bulging eyes, and his nose looked like someone had flattened it with a stone. He patiently listened to the man standing.

The younger man was complaining about his female relatives — fourteen in all — who had moved in with him because of all the recent political turmoil in Athens. The problem, which he explained at great length and in great detail, was that they were eating him out of house and home. He seemed quite agitated by the situation.

When the seated man began to speak, the crowd quieted down. He didn't sound at all like he looked. He sounded youthful, exuberant. He spoke so softly Pandora could barely hear him and had to move closer. The rhythm of his voice made her feel warm and safe. His words sounded like they were coated with honey. The more she listened, the more entranced she became.

He was gently "suggesting" that the standing man "might consider" putting his female relatives to work so that they could earn some money.

Pandora was stunned by this. In her whole life, she had never heard anything like it — except inside her own head. Up until now, she was certain she was the only person in Athens who thought such things.

The standing man laughed, considering this a most outlandish suggestion, perhaps even a joke.

Maybe he had not explained himself clearly. His relatives were not slaves but freeborn, aristocratic ladies and, therefore, not acquainted with work. Work was beneath them. They preferred to spend all day washing themselves and applying unguents.

The seated man was not put off by this. Indeed, he seemed to expect it. He admitted that this idea — that women could work and earn money — might appear at first to be most radical. But perhaps, if he took the time to think about it with a truly open mind, he would realize that it was possible that his female relatives would be happier if they earned some money so that they could contribute, rather than sit at home and be idle.

The standing man waved his hand at him, as if to say he had had enough, and he left.

The seated man rose up and slowly — he had an odd way of walking — made his way through the crowd, which parted as he proceeded.

He walked right past Pandora, so close that she could almost reach out and touch him. For some reason, he stopped just then, turned, and looked back at her. He walked back to her, and she could feel him looking at her. She was afraid to raise her eyes and look directly into his. She had never looked into any man's eyes outside of her family. She had no idea what might happen.

"What is your name, child?" he said sweetly. Someone said, "Pandora," although it wasn't just someone, it was her.

He laughed. It was a laugh that was different from any Pandora had ever heard. It was full of discovery and delight. Discovering that there was still something to laugh about after all these years. And delighted that life was full of little surprises like a girl who stood out from the crowd and had a name like Pandora.

Which is when he told her about the original Pandora. Just before he was shuttled away, he said, "A truly magnificent name, my child, but a heavy burden. I shall help you lift it. I will be here next week at this same time, and we will talk more then."

Of course, had Pandora known that the Wise One — for that is what she called him inside her head — was not the only person she would meet at the Fountain House who would change her life, she would have been even more thunderstruck.

PART
TWO

PART

TWO

A Sign From the Gods

Pandora became obsessed with the Wise One. Who was he? Where did he come from? What exactly was it that he was teaching? She desperately needed to find out as much as she could about him.

As driven as she was — and when Pandora set her mind to something she could be quite focused — she knew she still had to control herself. She knew she had to be discreet. No one in her family could know about the meeting at the fountain, not even her stepmother. And certainly not her father. If he were to find out, he would surely forbid her to ever go there again.

Hearing that Uncle Stephanos was coming to dinner that very night was, as far as Pandora was concerned, nothing less than a sign from the gods. It was an opportunity she was not about to waste.

Uncle Stephanos was her father's taller, older brother. He combined a dignified face, a curly head of hair, a neatly trimmed beard, and sparkling brown eyes. This, along with his ready wit and ample wealth, made him one of Athens's most sought-after widowers.

A great athlete in his younger days — he won the chariot race and boxed in the Olympic Games — Stephanos was even more well-known as a leading figure in Athenian politics.

Until his retirement the previous year, he was one of the nine chief magistrates of the city. When he left office, he was given a big banquet at the Prytaneum, where all of Athens's most distinguished citizens were honored.

He was spending more time now managing his vast land holdings, which included numerous, lucrative silver mines that needed hundreds and hundreds of slaves to function.

But he always made time for the four things he enjoyed most in life: eating (he once told Pandora that he wished he had the throat of a crane so that he could enjoy food for an even longer time); making music; telling stories; and being with his favorite niece, the joke being that Pandora was his only niece.

Pandora's uncle knew everyone in Athens; indeed it seemed as if he knew everyone in the world, Persia and Egypt included. He would know about the Wise One.

Normally Pandora and Charis didn't join Pandora's father when he had guests for dinner, other than to supervise the slaves who prepared and served the meal. But Uncle Stephanos was an exception. He insisted that the "ladies partake," as he put it. Her uncle was unlike anyone Pandora had ever met, although she hadn't met that many people. He danced to a different tune, one that he alone heard. He no longer accepted invitations to dinner, her house being the only place outside of his own that he dined. Pandora admired him greatly and wondered how it was that Menander was his son. Unfortunately he, too, was coming to dinner.

Pandora pondered for hours on end (time being one of the things she had plenty of) how it was that a father so intelligent and charming could have a son so witless. It was truly one of nature's mysteries.

And this wasn't just a theoretical dilemma, something Pandora conjured up to pass the time of day (though she could, at times, be accused of just that). No, in this instance the dilemma was real, for Menander had been chosen as her future husband. In only a year, Pandora would be fourteen, ripe for marriage.

Even though Pandora knew full well that it was unheard of for Athenian girls to choose their own husbands or to have any say in that matter at all, she tried to talk to her stepmother. Unfortunately her stepmother believed (or said she believed) that Menander was a "fine man" and "at thirty, just the right age for her." Alcander, she said, had "chosen well," and she was lucky to be marrying a first cousin. Her stepmother was sure they would have "many wonderful children together."

The conversation made Pandora realize just how much her stepmother had changed. Charis was no longer the feisty, independent Spartan woman she once was. She had slowly become, over the past eight years, a proper Athenian wife, concerned only with obeying and pleasing her husband.

Pandora wanted to ask her stepmother if she were aware that she had changed, but she was afraid that would hurt her feelings. She wanted to ask her if she was glad she had come all the way to Athens to be married. If it had been worth it. Pandora knew that marriage would not be enough for her.

Of course, Charis knew nothing of the talk among the slaves. They constantly made fun of Menander, saying he must have been adopted from a family in Boeotia because he was such a "fool" — that all he did was sit around all day and eat. They said that he had been born feetfirst, which, to some degree, explained his odd behavior.

Most recently they were talking about more serious matters, for example, how he was throwing away his father's money. Everyone respected Uncle Stephanos, as he was known to all because he treated his slaves better than most, gave food to the hungry, clothes to the elderly, and had no fences around his property so people could come and pick fruit. Menander was spending his money at a rapid pace. If he continued losing it betting on the horses, quail tipping, and at the Thursday night cockfights, he might actually succeed in wiping out their fortune.

Pandora knew about this because Thratta, a slave girl, told her everything the other slaves talked about.

The only thing she couldn't decide was which was a sillier waste of time, quail tipping or cockfighting.

She couldn't imagine sitting around for hours while a large circle was drawn around an innocent and unsuspecting quail, which was then hit on the head to see if it would stand its ground or back out of the circle — all while people placed bets.

Of course, cockfighting was even more unfathomable to Pandora. Why would anyone want to see these poor chickens, primed with garlic and onions to make them want to fight, their spurs tipped with bronze barbs so that each blow struck would result in even more bloodshed than usual?

What didn't surprise her was that Menander liked to spend his time this way. That's why she gave him her very own name: Meander, because he just seemed to wander aimlessly through life, following no road, heading toward no goal.

Peace Was
the Exception

✧ ✧ ✧

Uncle Stephanos arrived alone (Menander would be wandering in later) and early, as was his custom. That way Pandora and her uncle would have time for a lyre lesson. Recently they had been concentrating on Pandora's posture, which was something of a problem.

"You're as rigid as the statue of Athena in the Parthenon," her uncle said, trying unsuccessfully to make her laugh and therefore relax. Lately, relaxing, much to Pandora's constant frustration, was easier said than done.

"Don't keep your thighs glued together," he repeated until she finally heard him, gave in, and relaxed.

Pandora loved playing the ancient ballads in the

traditional way, just like her uncle taught her. He frowned on showy techniques such as too much tremolo.

When she first began her lessons, she used a small stick to strike the seven strings of the tortoiseshell lyre, which had been a present from him. But now her uncle allowed her to use her fingers, which had become supple and strong.

Sometimes, but only when she was feeling particularly confident (which was rare), she sang while he accompanied her on the double-reeded *aulos.* It amused her uncle that the *aulos,* which he had been playing since he was a boy, had become all the rage in Athens. Pandora liked the way it sounded — like the buzzing of wasps in the upper registers and honking of geese in the lower ones — but she didn't like the way it made her uncle's cheeks puff out while he played.

The lesson was briefer than usual because they were having roasted thrush with pureed beans and lentils, and Uncle Stephanos couldn't wait to eat.

Dinner began with a discussion about the death penalty — something the two brothers had been debating for months.

Alcander was very much in favor of the death

penalty; in fact, he thought that anyone who committed *any* crime should get the death penalty.

Uncle Stephanos made a gesture as if he had something wrong with his ears and couldn't possibly be hearing correctly. He asked Alcander if he advocated the death penalty even for petty crimes like stealing vegetables from the greengrocer in the agora.

Alcander prided himself on taking extreme positions and defending them no matter how absurd they were. As always, he was emboldened by the wine. All crimes, he said, petty or not, deserve the death penalty. He just couldn't think of any penalty that was worse to impose on those who committed more serious crimes.

This topic sputtered to an end with Pandora's good-natured uncle saying, "You never cease to amaze me, my little brother." Pandora was uncertain if he knew how much the "little" infuriated her father.

Next, of course, was the Long War. Pandora questioned if the war had taken as long to fight as it took her father to discuss.

It wasn't even that her father was all that patriotic. As far as she could tell, he wasn't — it was just that he liked talking about the war.

Pandora hated listening to any political discussions, least of all talk about war. Alcander seemed to enjoy talking about how terrible it was, how brutal it was. How the fighting just seemed to go on forever. To her it sounded as though the war had been going on since the beginning of time. That peace was the exception, not the rule. It had been five years since Sparta had finally defeated Athens. To hear her father talking you would have thought it was yesterday.

Her father explained, yet again — to whom, she didn't know; they had all heard it so many times and even her brother looked bored — how everyone had to abandon their homes; how they all had to retreat behind the protective walls of the inner city, leaving the farms for the invading Spartan army to burn but giving them no people to kill. Athenians had endured extreme crowding and discomfort even before the angry gods had sent the plague to punish them and kill one out of every three citizens of Athens.

Alcander told the same story he always did. About how his ship was manned and ready to leave when a sudden eclipse of the sun turned day into night. Everyone considered it an ill omen.

It was always unclear, no matter how many times

Pandora heard the story, but it seemed that her father never left Athens during the war.

A welcome sign that Alcander was winding down was his listing causes of the war. Unlike all the other times, however, her uncle spoke up at the end.

"Greed caused the war, my brother. Greed is the cause of all war."

＊

Once, when Pandora was alone at her uncle's house, she saw his shield leaning up against a wall. She ran her fingers over its cold, hard, smooth surface and tried to lift it but couldn't — just touching it frightened her.

She was thankful that war was men's business, that being a soldier was left to the boys.

Dutifully and Duplicitously

⚹　　⚹　　⚹

Pandora was so restless and bored she was actually glad when Meander meandered in late, as usual.

He had just come from a visit to his oculist because of a bothersome eye infection, which he displayed for everyone at the table after wiping his hands to make sure his fingers were clean. The oculist recommended he bathe the eye once a day and, at night, apply a salve he gave him. Meander seemed much relieved to hear that the eye infection wasn't life threatening.

His health — the aches, pains, and ailments he had, of which there were many, and the treatments he was taking to remedy them — was (along with his pet jackdaw, whom he was training to walk up and down a ladder carrying a miniature sword) one of Meander's favorite topics.

He was forever talking about the various ointments, including one of his new concoctions — goat fat and fig tree juice — which he was finding effective for a great number of, as he called them, "eruptions" (something Pandora was looking forward to hearing nothing further about).

But Meander's most favorite topic was hunting. As he began, Pandora considered if it were possible that a grave error had been made and Meander was really her father's child and she her uncle's. She also fretted about when and how she was going to get the conversation to go where she wanted it to go.

Meander told everyone about some recent success he was having with his bow and arrow, how much fun it was hunting birds with a slingshot, and how adept he had become at impaling hares with a stick.

Then he lectured Pandora on how to dig and construct a pit trap, something that, just from the sound of it, held absolutely no interest for her.

Pandora had to sit there for what seemed like forever, hearing how the pit had to be deep enough so that the sides were sheer; how you covered the opening with branches and leaves ("camouflaging" it, Meander explained, saying the word slowly, as if the word was much too complicated for Pandora's lowly female nature to comprehend); how you had to stake a lamb at the bottom of the pit (at this point, Pandora had to fight the urge to stop her ears, stand up, and scream, "Please be quiet or I will go mad!") so the lamb will cry out and attract the prey, who would then crash down through the thin canopy covering.

"That's all there is to it," Meander said smugly, looking as if he had just invented the sundial.

Dutifully, Pandora gave him an appropriately admiring look.

The Only Road to True Happiness

The Only Road to True Happiness

⚘   ⚘   ⚘

Patience was not Pandora's most out-standing quality. To a large degree it was a characteristic she was, by nature, unfamiliar with. Any patience she appeared to possess was imposed on her from the outside, not felt from within.

But she knew she had to be patient now. She knew she had to wait for the right moment. She couldn't simply *ask*. The mere fact that she spoke at all at the dinner table would call enough attention to her. Her stepmother, who used to speak occasionally, now spoke very little. Pandora didn't want anyone to become suspicious. Someone would have to say something so that Pandora, with an innocent word or two placed just so, could gently push the conversation in the proper direction.

When Polybius started talking about Lysias, his teacher, Pandora knew her chance was coming.

Still she waited, yet again suffering silently as her brother described his class; the other pupils; their uncomfortable, backless stools; and his teacher's thronelike chair.

It was now or never.

Speaking almost in a whisper and looking only at her brother, she inquired, most humbly, if his teacher had heard about this old man who was seen speaking in the district recently. At least, that's what she had heard from Apollonia. He was a teacher of some sort, according to Apollonia. . . .

It worked; everyone took the bait.

Her uncle was even more familiar with the Wise One's teaching than she had hoped.

For one thing he had a name — Socrates. In his youth, he had been a stonemason and a sculptor but soon turned to teaching philosophy as a vocation.

He was quite unconventional: He refused to take students, giving no private lessons, having no regular schedule or classroom — preferring street corners to lecture halls. He wrote nothing — no treatise, no books. Not a word was written down.

According to Socrates, her uncle explained,

books can't be questioned, corrected, or further re-fined like a conversation. Uncle Stephanos indicated clearly by his manner of speech and the tone of his voice that, although he respected and admired the man in general, here was an area where they didn't see eye-to-eye.

Socrates was trying, unlike other teachers, to make people think for themselves and not just follow what anyone tells them is true. He urged anyone who chose to listen to him — he claimed he had no students, no followers — not to concern themselves with mundane, practical matters. Their time was better spent on perfecting their souls.

This, he said, was the only road to true happiness.

Polybius added that his teacher had known Socrates quite well over the years. He found his practices most curious: refusing to charge anything for his teaching, claiming that he was ignorant and therefore his teachings had no monetary value. Lysias said it was a shame because he could earn quite a good salary.

Pandora kept one eye on her father throughout the discussion — she always kept one eye on her father.

She had never seen the two brothers agree on

anything. Alcander was clearly jealous of his older brother's success. He always took the opposite position on whatever view his brother had. And now was no different. It was as if they were talking about two different men.

She could see that her father had gotten his second wind. There would be no stopping him now.

This Socrates was an old fool who talked to anyone and everyone about anything that popped into his head, which was permanently ensconced in the clouds rather than back here on Earth. He spent his whole day simply wasting his and everyone else's time, conducting discussions that led nowhere and concluded nothing. He talked nonsense and asked ridiculous questions such as "What is courage?" as if everyone didn't know, or "Why do good people do bad things?" as if anyone cared. He told one and all how to live their lives when he couldn't figure out his own. His wife was a real nag, which was why he didn't spend any time at home with his children. He didn't have a drachma to his name and couldn't afford to buy a decent pair of sandals so he went about barefoot all day long.

He was a destructive influence on children today, Alcander continued. He headed an evil cult, twisting the young minds of those who followed him blindly. He taught them to ignore the gods who protect the citizens of Athens and to invent their own deities. He taught them to be disrespectful of their fathers and attacked the very moral fiber of the family.

"He's a subversive who is creating a generation of troublemakers, hoodlums, and revolutionaries," Alcander concluded.

Pandora had to suppress a smile. The angrier her father grew, the more pronounced his lisp became.

Living on the Stars

✤   ✤   ✤

Alcander fell asleep right there, where he was already nearly fully reclined, on the dining room couch. Polybius excused himself to study, and Meander drifted off into the night without even saying good-bye. Since it was Thursday, Pandora assumed he was going to attend the cockfights.

Happily, this left only Pandora and Charis to listen to Uncle Stephanos's after-dinner story. All three secretly liked it that way, of course, never saying anything to the others; they looked forward to what had become a welcome ritual. As they settled in on the front terrace, overlooking the hill, they nibbled on nuts, dried fruit, and figs. Pandora smelled the sweet night air and stared up at the stars. If the

gods lived on Mount Olympus, what fantastic creatures were living on the stars?

She hoped tonight's story wouldn't be as frightening as the one about the woman who chose to bite
off her tongue rather than reveal a secret.

That story scared Pandora so much she had bad
dreams for many nights after.

Still worse, not only because it was so sad but
even more because it was true, was the story about
Uncle Stephanos's dog. He had found her, an unwanted, abandoned pup and had raised her himself.

It had all happened during the Long War. The
dog was eight then but "still as lively as the day I
found her." Uncle Stephanos was going off to fight
the Spartans. "I was much younger then, but not
nearly as handsome as I am today." He bid farewell
to family and friends, boarded his trireme, and
sailed off.

No one heard the sound of her furious, frantic
barking over the noise made by the pounding surf.
Distraught over his master's leave-taking, the dog
had leaped into the sea and attempted to follow him
wherever it was he might be going.

They found her soaked, limp, exhausted body

washed back up on the same shore in the morning. Pandora's uncle didn't find out until two years later. He had been a prisoner of war and was only released after a ransom was paid.

She now rested in her very own tomb on her master's estate.

⚜

"Tonight's story," Stephanos began in his melodious stage voice, "is about Argeia, a Theban woman who was married to King Aristodemus many, many years ago.

"After Argeia joyously gave birth to twin boys her husband died quite unexpectedly. It became, therefore, most imperative — certainly as far as his numerous relatives were concerned (he seemed to have more now that he was dead) — that the mother reveal which one of the twins had been the firstborn so that he could be declared the rightful heir and everyone could, of course, scramble around as best they could to win over the new, rich, infant heir.

"Argeia refused to do this.

"The eager relatives, however, were not to be denied. They watched her every move, without her knowing. She was never out of their sight. Finally, they got what they wanted. They ascertained that she always bathed one of the boys before the other, and it was decided that he must be the eldest and, therefore, the rightful heir, and he was crowned accordingly."

Pandora was relieved that the story wasn't scary or sad. She never knew with Uncle Stephanos — "Unpredictability is part of my charm," he liked to say and, indeed, it was.

⚮

Pandora went to bed feeling more content than she had felt in a long, long time.

She was counting the days until she would see the Wise One again. She hoped he would remember her. The possibility that he wouldn't had never crossed her mind until that very moment. He *had* to remember. He was just what she was looking for, although up until that very moment she wasn't aware that she had been looking for anything.

PART
THREE

A Most Reliable Cure

Although she didn't say anything to anyone or give any outward indication, Charis had grown quite concerned about her stepdaughter's recent bad dreams and her odd behavior.

She gently brought up the subject of the nightmares and Pandora said, with apparent sincerity, that they were the result of Uncle Stephanos's stories. Although Charis had herself spent many sleepless nights after hearing one of his stories, somehow she felt that was not the real reason for her stepdaughter's troubling behavior.

It wasn't that Pandora wasn't helpful around the house, or that she wasn't respectful. It was just that she had become so secretive and seemed so agitated and preoccupied. Her mind always seemed to be someplace else, someplace far, far away. She seemed so unsettled, was how her stepmother thought of it.

For quite a while Charis tried to convince herself that she was worrying needlessly and seeing more than there was. She tended to do that. But every time she convinced herself that she was just imagining it, Pandora would do something to confirm her suspicions.

Like the girl's behavior at dinner. It was subtle, nothing she could really put her finger on, but Pandora just wasn't herself lately. Something had to be done.

She decided to consult a physician.

She didn't ask her husband — she knew he wouldn't allow it. But there was still enough of the Spartan woman left in her to do what she thought was right.

Charis told Thratta to make sure the doctor came the next morning because she knew Pandora would be away visiting Apollonia and helping her and her mother with her brand-new baby sister.

The physician arrived, talking to himself, it appeared, about a love potion he had recently recommended that wasn't working and a patient who had died from the effects of a horse bite. Charis told him everything she had observed about Pandora's condition. She hoped that the keener her observations were, the more accurately and effectively he could prescribe a remedy. She told him about the fevers, the faraway look in Pandora's eyes, the nervous energy, and the nightmares.

He asked her to be specific about the nightmares, but she could only remember the last two, both of which were so disturbing that Pandora came into her bed.

She told him about the one where the huge eagle swooped down from the sky and wrapped Pandora up in its great wingspan; lifted her up; and took her on a long, long journey to a land she had never heard of.

And she told him about the horrible night that Pandora dreamed she had a snake curled up inside her, and how it had begun working its way up her throat, attempting to get out. It was Pandora's job not to allow this. No matter what, she had to prevent the snake from escaping. It had to remain buried deep within her so it could not harm anyone else.

Much to her surprise, the physician assured Charis that she had absolutely nothing to worry about. He had no doubt what the problem was, and not only that, he was able to prescribe a most reliable cure.

He wasn't surprised that the girl was having fevers and nightmares. As a matter of fact, given Pandora's age, he wasn't surprised by any of the symptoms. They were quite common, which was a relief to Pandora's stepmother; she had hoped that since the symptoms were quite common the cure would be simple enough.

"In fact," the physician rambled on rapidly and absentmindedly, he had "seen a number of cases just like it recently." One girl — despite her mother's having a swing constructed to help calm her nerves — had just thrown herself down a well in despair and drowned. Seeing the panic that now consumed Pandora's stepmother's already troubled countenance, the good doctor backtracked furiously, emphasizing that it was a "most difficult case" with "grave complications," and there were factors that he was not at liberty to discuss that didn't pertain here. Her stepdaughter's case was much simpler, much more straightforward.

"Blood flow," that was the problem. The blood was probably flowing up to Pandora's heart and lungs, causing the fever and the nightmares. There was no doubt. He had seen it before, hundreds of times, maybe thousands, the doctor said with a chuckle.

Marriage, that was the only solution, and the sooner the better. Pandora's stepmother was relieved that the solution was so simple.

"The sooner the better," he repeated, and went on. "The sooner girls your stepdaughter's age get married and bear children, the sooner they can be rid of these dreadful symptoms."

Charis thanked the learned physician most earnestly. She was greatly relieved and considered herself most fortunate. Relieved because there was medical help for Pandora's condition and fortunate that her forthcoming marriage to Menander was already in the planning stages.

All that had to be done now was to make sure the wedding took place sooner rather than later. The wedding date would have to be moved up to Gamelin, the seventh month, a good month, since it was the sacred month for Hera, the goddess of marriage.

It would be, Charis thought, the least she could do for the daughter she had come to love as her very own.

The Silence Filled the Rooms

The Silence Filled the Rooms

✤　✤　✤

While walking to Apollonia's house that very same morning, Pandora was thinking about childbirth. She thought about it long and hard. The truth was she was not looking forward to it, something she never mentioned to anyone. She knew it was a disgraceful thought, and she tried to stop it from coming into her head, but she just couldn't.

And the entire process took much, much too long. Apollonia's mother was ill and had headaches for *months*. She had ivy sickness almost the whole time, eating everything, especially cheese omelettes. Everyone was thankful she didn't eat earth and coal like her sister did when she was pregnant, leading to the mark on her child's head.

Just hearing Appolonia's mother talk about her

trials with fertility testing was more than enough for
Pandora. Hearing how she had to breathe in fumi-
gations of crushed laurel leaves, wormwood, beeswax,
sulphur, and garlic. And the part about being
wrapped in a cloak and having burning incense
placed under her. Waiting anxiously to see if the
smell of the incense passed through her body and
could be smelled on her breath. Hoping that it did
because this would confirm that she was indeed able
to bear children.

But that was only the beginning.

When, at last, the gods smiled on Apollonia's
family and the hydromel that the midwife gave to
her mother to drink did indeed cause colic in her
stomach, they were certain she was carrying a child.

The question was, boy or girl?

After two girls, Apollonia's father wanted a boy.

Throughout the pregnancy everyone said that the
baby would be a girl because Apollonia's mother's
complexion was so bad. She ate as much roast veal as
she could, hoping that would help insure the birth
of a boy.

As they got closer to the birth, Pandora helped
them smear the house with pitch to keep away evil
spirits.

Pandora deeply regretted her decision to see the baby being born, but Apollonia had insisted. She watched, utterly transfixed, as the midwife prepared, getting the birthing stool ready and making sure her fingernails were cut short enough.

Apollonia's family, although not actually poor, didn't have nearly as much money as Pandora's. Apollonia's father was a farmer and had recently shut down his shield factory, which he maintained as a sideline. Their house was small, and they could only employ two slaves. The girl slave helped the midwife with the birth.

Pandora had never seen anything so messy and painful in her life. Apollonia's mother looked so disheveled and haggard when it was over that it only confirmed what Pandora already knew. It wasn't for her.

She could never say anything about this to her stepmother. Even if she agreed with Pandora or sympathized just a little, she would never say it. She would have to keep up appearances. But Pandora remembered, years ago, before Charis had changed, when Apollonia's mother was pregnant with Apollonia's sister. Then Pandora's stepmother said she would rather go into battle than give birth.

Her stepmother ended up having a family, and she didn't have to give birth, Pandora thought, as she arrived at Apollonia's house.

She was rather surprised that Apollonia was not in her usual position, leaning in the doorway, watching the road for passersby. Apollonia was, if this were possible, even more bored than Pandora and that was one of the ways she liked to pass the time.

Pandora thought she was probably too busy inside with her newest baby sister.

Pandora noticed the silence even before she stepped across the threshold. In the past two days, the baby had been crying out constantly, her plaintive pleas filling the house. Now the only sound was of the dogs barking and silence filled the rooms.

Pandora whispered as loud as she dared, "Apollonia."

There was no one around. They could be upstairs, in the women's quarters, but the baby would have been downstairs, where the water was.

Again Pandora whispered, "Apollonia, Apollonia." In the quiet, it sounded as though she were shouting, but she knew she wasn't. The silence was everywhere, heavy and dark.

Apollonia scared her. Pandora almost tripped over her friend, crouched in a darkened corner, bundled up in her cloak, even though it wasn't cold. She was furiously carding a basket of wool, her pet dove perched on her shoulder as usual.

"Where's the baby?" Pandora asked, sensing as soon as the words left her mouth that she wasn't sure she wanted to hear the answer.

"Gone," Apollonia said simply, as if that were enough.

"Gone where?" Pandora whispered.

Apollonia didn't say anything for quite a while, and Pandora obeyed her instinct to remain quiet.

Finally, Apollonia spoke.

Her father had been unhappy that it was yet another girl. He didn't even want the garlands of spun wool hung on the door to announce the birth of a girl. It wasn't to exist; it had to be abandoned.

Apollonia's mother asked him to make sure the baby was left in a place where someone might come along and take it home with them.

Her father had the slave girl wrap the baby in a shawl and take it to the road that led to Piraeus Harbor and lay it on the ground there.

Something Left to Be Said

⚓ ⚓ ⚓

Pandora thought the day would never come.

She had to fight the temptation to leave as soon as she awoke in the morning. She knew that would be foolish for two reasons. One, it would make her stepmother suspicious. It was most unlike Pandora to go to the Fountain House before the late afternoon, when the most people would be there. Her stepmother would notice. And lately, she had been giving Pandora funny looks, as though something were on her mind.

But the most important reason was that Pandora wanted to be there at exactly the same time she had been the week before.

The day just dragged on and on. No matter what

she did to make it go quicker, it refused to co-operate.

Pandora spent most of the morning in her room, daydreaming, rearranging things (although there wasn't much to rearrange), and idly playing with toys she had from when she was younger: her knucklebones, a top, her rattle and terra-cotta dolls, hoops, a yo-yo, a tambourine, and a horse on wheels. She even found her baby bottle and potty seat, which amused her.

She wanted to see if she could still juggle her balls as well as she used to, and she was gratified to see that she could.

Then she helped her stepmother do some things around the house before she went back to her room, put on her wool fleece, and bathed in perfumed oils. It was almost time.

Just before she left for the Fountain House, she took her ivory comb and a ribbon so she could fix up her hair on the way. She wanted to make a good impression on the Wise One.

⚓

When Pandora arrived at the Fountain House, there was no crowd, just the same faces she always saw, coming and going at a snail's pace, lazily passing the time of day. Nothing like the buzz that was in the air from the moment she had arrived last week.

The Wise One was nowhere to be seen.

She decided to sit and wait on the same rock he had been sitting on when he talked to the man about his relatives.

After what seemed like quite a while, Pandora, forgetting her water vessel, began the long uphill climb back home.

She was walking past a low-lying shrub, thinking about, of all things, how funny it was that Uncle Stephanos refused to eat onions because he said he was on the lookout for a new wife, even though it was so obvious that he wasn't.

She heard someone call her name but thought she must have been imagining it so she continued on her way. But then, there it was again: "Pandora."

She turned around, and the most beautiful boy she had ever seen was standing behind the bush and looking at her, saying nothing.

He had blue, blue eyes, a nose that would have been perfect if it hadn't been slightly off center, puffy lips, and very, very curly black hair.

Then he did the oddest thing: He fainted. Just like that, crumpling down behind the bush and disappearing from sight.

Pandora scrambled to where he had fallen, lifted his head, and felt that it was beaded with hot sweat. It was clear he was suffering from a raging fever.

She ran back to the fountain, dipped the hem of her cloak into the cool water, and laid it on his fevered forehead, letting it remain there until he opened his eyes.

"I must have fainted," he said.

"You did," she said.

"I'm fine now," he said, already brushing off the dust from his tunic, wanting to forget the incident.

He seemed content to just stand there and say nothing. Pandora had never seen a face so helpless and sweet. It was, however, apparent that Pandora would have to do the leading if they were going to get anywhere.

"Did you call me?" Pandora asked, trying to sound like his reluctance to speak wasn't making her as uncomfortable as it was.

"Yes," the boy said, but only after a while, as if he were thinking about something else, although he never took his eyes off her.

She hoped he would elaborate, but he didn't. It was as if the "yes" was a completely informative answer and nothing else was necessary.

Pandora pressed on.

"Why?" she inquired, growing impatient with the slow pace of the conversation.

"Why, what?" he said, causing Pandora to wonder if he were playing a game with her or joking. At this pace, she wouldn't be home before dark.

"Why did you call my name?" she said a little condescendingly.

"To invite you to a party," he said, as if it were the most commonplace thing in the world.

But to Pandora it was worlds away from commonplace; it was the most outrageous thing anyone had ever said to her. She barely knew what a party was other than the parties her father and brother attended until all hours, both staggering home drunk and falling asleep on the terrace.

"He sends his regrets," the boy continued. "He has unavoidably been detained, attending to some unpleasant legal business, although he would have much rather kept his appointment with you. He is most grievously sorry and hopes you will accept his apologies.

"He has sent me in his stead and urges you to accept his invitation to the party, three nights hence, at Cleon's house."

Pandora didn't know if she were more stunned than confused. The more she heard, the less she understood. She asked him the first thing that came to her mind.

"Didn't only men go to these parties, besides women who . . ." She let her voice trail off, not really knowing how to say what she wanted to say.

Her question, it seemed, had been anticipated.

"Socrates suggests that perhaps you could consider cutting your hair like a boy's and attending with me — as friends. That way you wouldn't look out of place. Socrates believes you would benefit greatly from attending and hearing the discussions."

This suggestion was even more astonishing to Pandora than the original invitation.

The boy, who had found both his tongue and his wits, described Socrates's plan in full.

After retiring to bed the night of the party, Pandora could cut her hair, climb out of her bedroom window, and down the fig tree. It would be a full moon, helping with the difficulties of seeing in the dark. He would be waiting on the downward slope of the hill and would take her to Socrates and the party.

Pandora's mind reeled. How did they know there was fig tree growing just outside her bedroom window? She didn't know what to say, so she said yes.

This pleased the boy greatly, and he smiled for the first time. But he continued to stand there, looking at her, just as he had throughout the entire conversation.

He looked as if there were still something left to be said, which, as it turns out, there was.

"Socrates was right," the boy said. "You are the most beautiful girl the gods ever created."

Like She Was
Feeling Nothing

The night of the party Pandora carefully prepared everything she would need: her bronze mirror, her comb, and the knife she had taken earlier from the kitchen.

She lay in bed waiting for the sounds that would tell her that her stepmother had settled in for the evening. Her father was out as usual, and Polybius had been in his room downstairs all evening, studying — not even bothering to eat.

It was a cloudless night, and the moonlight was streaming in through her bedroom window, casting an eerie blue glow on all it touched: her bed, the oil lamp, the chair, her hands, everything. It reminded her of the last time the sky was cloudless and the moon was full.

It was the night of her mother's funeral. Pandora was being torn apart by her grief. She was feeling so sad it was as if she felt nothing.

The memories were vivid — they haunted her to this day — but they were fragmented. She remembered overhearing plans: Her mother had to be dressed in her clean, white, burial shroud. Rings and bracelets had to be picked out, some for her to wear and others to be buried with her. Her body had to be anointed with oils and perfumes and surrounded with sweet-smelling herbs.

Pandora could hear the excitement in the women's voices. She knew, even back then, that funerals were one of the very few outdoor activities women were allowed to attend, hence the excitement. Some even talked about how grateful they were to get some sun and fresh air, as if her dying were a final gift Pandora's mother was bestowing on them.

She heard them talking about the *obol* they placed in her mother's mouth so she could pay the ferryman for her passage across the river Styx. This confused Pandora. There were no ferries near their house. And just as confusing was why they were placing honey cakes in the coffin for a watchdog who oversaw Hades. She had never heard of Hades.

Pandora remembered things she saw that day: the women closing her mother's eyes and putting on the chin straps that held her jaw in place. Washing her body and then laying her in her coffin, scattering ashes in her hair, and wreathing her head in flowers before resting it on a pillow. She saw the slaves shading her mother from the sunlight and shooing away flies with fans, and she wondered why. Surely her poor mother was no longer bothered by the sun's rays or the annoying flies.

It seemed as if her mother remained in the house for weeks, but really it was only two days.

She remembered her mother's coffin being carried on the slaves' shoulders and hoping that they wouldn't drop it and then watching as they carefully slid it onto the waiting wagon. How forlorn the mules look, she had thought.

She remembered the funeral procession. The men walking in front of the wagon and Pandora and the rest of the women walking behind.

She didn't remember anything from the cemetery other than the sound of the flutes mixing hideously with the cries and shrieks coming from women she barely knew who tore at their hair.

She watched while her father purified the house

with hyssop and placed a jar of water outside the door so people passing would know there had been a death within and those arriving could sprinkle the water on themselves to prevent contamination.

The last thing Pandora remembered was what was written on her mother's tomb, the tomb she visited without fail every morning:

PENELOPE LIES IN HER TOMB
WHEN SHE WAS ALIVE HER HUSBAND AND
   CHILDREN LOVED HER
WHEN SHE WAS DEAD SHE WAS LAMENTED.

Pandora hadn't known what *lament* meant then, but she did now.

A Nice Feeling

The boy held the mirror tentatively but dutifully obeyed Pandora's commands to turn it this way and that. There was enough moonlight for her to see that he was even more handsome than she remembered but not enough for her to cut her hair properly. One side ended up longer than the other, and she could feel a hole in the back where she had cut it too short. She had wanted him to do the back, but he shook his head violently, as if she had asked him to tame a wild beast.

It was shocking to see how easily she could look like a boy, as if the difference were just in the length of the hair.

He insisted on holding her hand all the way

down the hill, citing the steepness and its rocky nature. Pandora's protests that she walked the hill every day of her life were ignored. The hill was steep, Pandora thought, but not *that* steep.

She was relieved that he was, at last, talking like a regular person, his raging fever having, obviously, subsided. He even told her his name, Phoenix.

On the way he said that the Wise One thought it best she stay close to him.

When they arrived the Wise One winked, acknowledging the secret that was between them. Then the slaves unwrapped the straps of Pandora's sandals from around her legs and washed her feet so she and Phoenix could enter the banquet room.

Everyone was dressed quite elegantly, some in fine linen robes and some with garlands of flowers on their heads and around their necks.

There were some women, and they looked and dressed exactly like the fashionable ladies Pandora had seen years ago in the cobbler's shop. One wore beautiful rosette-shaped earrings and another a bracelet around her ankle. Even though the party had hardly started, the guests seemed quite relaxed, lying around on cushions and bolsters.

The slaves brought in basins of water for every-one to wash their hands so their fingers would be clean enough to eat with. Then they placed the food on the small, round tables that were arranged in front of the couches on the raised, stone platform in the center of the room.

Pandora was surprised by the bad table manners displayed by some of the guests. Most ate their fresh fish with two fingers and wiped their soiled hands on their bread, as was proper, but some didn't bother with such niceties.

After dinner, the slaves cleared the tables, lit the incense burners, and swept the floor, which was lit-tered with discarded bread crusts and meat bones (hurriedly gobbled up by two dogs, who darted away when the perfumed water was splashed on the floor).

Phoenix explained to Pandora that now the main part of the evening, the serious drinking and talk-ing, could begin.

New guests arrived, not caring to come for din-ner but wanting to be present for the discussions that followed.

The slaves poured the wine through a sieve, re-moving the little bits of grape and the vine debris, added water, and poured it into the individual drinking cups that had been passed around.

The cups were much smaller than the two-handled ones her father drank from. And the scenes painted on them weren't at all like the scenes depicted on the ones at home.

Phoenix explained that they drank from small cups at the beginning of the party and progressed to bigger ones as the night wore on, which seemed backward to Pandora.

One man joked that the potters were making the cups so precious these days that maybe people weren't supposed to drink from them but just look at them. Then he made fun of how elegantly you had to drink from the dainty little things.

Some of the guests wanted to switch to the bigger cups right away, now that the eating was over. But Socrates insisted that they stay with the small ones a while longer.

"The wine is to loosen our tongues and free our minds so we might converse in an enlightened manner," he said like an angry but understanding parent scolding his young children.

Some of the guests wanted to play *kottabos*. The slaves set up the big bowl, filled it with wine, and floated saucers in it. Then the players tried to toss enough wine from the cups and whoever sank the largest number of saucers was declared the winner.

While all this was going on, there was entertainment. A boy played the kithara, an acrobat juggled a dozen rings at a time, and flute girls performed. To Pandora, they seemed rather exotically dressed for girls who were just playing the flute.

Some of the guests recited poetry and some told stories. One, about a middle-of-the-day marriage, was a real crowd pleaser. Pandora didn't understand what a middle-of-the-day marriage was nor why it was so funny. But parts of the story she did understand, and it made her blush.

That must have been the reason Phoenix put his arm around her waist.

It was a nice feeling, she thought.

Pandora had been feeling rather nice ever since Phoenix brought her the second cup of wine. She had never tasted wine before — her father strictly forbid it. Even smelling the dark burgundy liquid made her a little dizzy.

She sipped tentatively at first.

THE PERPETUAL SEEKING
OF WISDOM

⚜   ⚜   ⚜

Some of the guests wanted to change places, so they could be as close to Socrates as possible. Socrates adamantly refused to show any favoritism, although he was besieged with requests to intervene.

In the back of the large room, there was quite a commotion when a man had his drinking cup knocked from his hand by one of the flute girls, who was sitting on his lap. It shattered into tiny pieces, which someone pointed out was a bad omen. It meant that one of his friends or a member of his family would soon die.

Socrates then sent the flute girls away, much to everyone's displeasure. He complimented his host and thanked him for "a delicious dinner and delightful entertainment."

A newcomer, who appeared to be quite drunk, called out to Socrates, asking him why he didn't charge anything for his teachings like all the other rhetoric teachers in Athens.

Socrates took great exception to being called a teacher of rhetoric and explained the difference at some length, summing up at the end: Rhetoric was the sport of winning an argument, and philosophy, which was what he practiced — carefully avoiding the word *teacher* — was the art of the perpetual seeking of wisdom.

Once you accept money, Socrates went on heatedly, you are obliged to talk to whomever is paying you and not say anything that might offend them and therefore jeopardize your finances.

"I cherish my independence. I talk to whomever I please and say whatever I please. By taking a fee, I would be selling my independence to the highest bidder."

Pandora could see that the Wise One felt deeply about this. He continued, a particular passion evident in his voice.

"Just look around you," he said. "Today men

rise to power strictly because of the money they have and the access to the people it brings. They address the multitudes with their fancy, empty speeches — speeches that are like honey cakes: sweet and palatable but lacking substance and, therefore, unhealthy in the long run."

Socrates paused, lost in reflection, and the discussion moved on.

During the discussion, people continued to drink and change couches for one reason or another.

Pandora and Phoenix took advantage of the situation and moved closer so that they could hear the Wise One better.

There was so much to think about. And Pandora was fascinated just watching the Wise One. She could see how completely consumed he was. He had become transformed — there was an otherworldly quality about him.

Pandora was eager to learn and thirsty for knowledge. How thirsty she hadn't been fully aware of until that moment. As she moved closer she felt like a parched woman crawling over desert sands toward an oasis.

Everyone wanted to discuss a play that all of Athens was talking about. It was written by Euripides, of whom Pandora, of course, had never heard — although the play sounded most provocative.

One of the guests stood up and recited from memory one of the female protagonist Medea's speeches.

"We women are the most unfortunate creatures.
Firstly, with an excess of wealth it is required
For us to buy a husband and take for our bodies
A master; for not to take one is even worse.
And now the question is serious whether we take
A good one or bad one; for there is no easy
escape. . . ."

Pandora was shocked to hear all of this and even more astonished to hear what the next topic of conversation was: Amazons. Amazons were women who lived a long, long time ago on the shores of the Black Sea. Somehow, they managed to live without men, hunting, fishing, and if necessary, fighting to protect themselves.

In order to procreate, they met men periodically in the mountains. If female babies resulted, they kept them; and if they were male, they gave them back to the men.

Amazons could understand the language that men spoke, but men could not understand the language that Amazons spoke, which made a great deal of sense to Pandora.

Socrates had not participated in this part of the discussion. He appeared to be lost in thought. Now, however, he returned, announcing that it was time to turn their attention to other matters.

"Like what?" someone shouted out, and Socrates stroked his long, white beard, rolled his eyes, and tilted his head toward the ceiling, as if he hadn't, until then, given any thought to the question and was looking to the heavens for divine inspiration.

"Aha," Socrates exclaimed, as though he had *finally* stumbled on the perfect topic. "How about the truth. How do we know the truth?"

This provoked, as obviously it was intended to, a lively discussion.

At first, they talked about words, how we use them and whether or not we understand their true meaning. Does talking effectively communicate what we want it to?

Then there was much discussion about wisdom and virtue. According to Socrates, virtue was knowledge. If someone knew, really knew, in their heart of hearts, that something was wrong, they wouldn't do it.

This was why, Socrates said, people were so dedicated to denying the truth to themselves. That way they could convince themselves that it was virtuous to charge a fortune for a pair of sandals.

Virtue, he concluded, was knowledge of what was truly good. And this allowed you to change your life for the better.

⚜

Some of the guests began to leave and some had to be helped home. Others had already fallen asleep right where they were.

One of the guests warned people not to go to sleep before they had vomited sufficiently and suggested that taking a light bath was a good idea. No one appeared to be paying him any mind.

Her Mind Was Elsewhere

Her Mind Was
Elsewhere

In the morning was the matter of her hair.

Pandora's father was sullen and angry beyond words. He stared at her for what seemed an endless amount of time, shook his head, and left the house.

Her brother, who had initially not reacted, wanting to see which way the wind blew, burst into a laughing fit and literally rolled around on the floor.

Her stepmother, her eyes cast down, said nothing.

Life went on just as it had before, but Pandora's mind was elsewhere.

She hardly heard a word her father said when he told them that his friend — the one who always dressed in rags to avoid paying taxes — had been arrested. Not for the taxes but for stealing public water and diverting it for his own use. Alcander found it terribly humorous that the jury accepted his plea. He claimed that his extravagant wife had made him do it. That he was totally henpecked, and although he was aware of it, couldn't help it. The jury dismissed his case, ruling that since he was acting under the influence of a woman, he was legally incompetent.

Pandora barely noticed when her father yelled at her for throwing the corn to the doves. When he asked her if she realized that corn was scarce because of the drought, her uncomprehending, blank stare angered him even more.

Even the debate between her brother and his newfound fellow students didn't annoy her.

The boys were debating a problem posed by their teacher. If a competitor in the Pentathlon accidentally hits another competitor with a javelin, killing him, who should be held accountable? The one who threw the javelin; the people who organized and put on the games; or the javelin itself?

In the past, Pandora, had she a javelin handy, might have ended the debate, but now the thought didn't even cross her mind.

Even the gossip among the slaves, which previously interested her more than anything else, didn't merit her attention.

And when the weasel caught yet another mouse, causing quite a commotion, she didn't even stir from her chair. While everyone ran around frantically and needlessly, Pandora just sat in a nearly catatonic state.

Only when Uncle Stephanos came for dinner, did she return, to some degree, to Earth. And even that was only because he said something to her during her lesson: "I guess you don't want to make music with me this evening."

Uncle Stephanos's story that night was brief. It was about the land of Sybaris. The people there lived in the lap of luxury, partying all night and sleeping all day. The Sybarites even went so far as to ban roosters from the town so they wouldn't be woken up by the crowing. They enjoyed eating so much that their chefs were their most honored citizens. They even taught their horses to dance. Once they were defeated in battle because of it. Their opponents played a tune on their flutes that lured the horses and, therefore, their cavalry away from the battle.

When her uncle left, Pandora returned to her thoughts about her weekly trips to the Fountain House. It was the second-most important thing in her life. The first was Phoenix, for she knew now that he was the boy she was going to marry.

RIGHT TO THE POINT

⚓ ⚓ ⚓

The next day, Pandora was relieved to see, as soon as she got halfway down the hill and over the last little rocky crest, that the Wise One and Phoenix were already at the Fountain House. She was breathless, not only from the arduous journey but from anticipation.

The crowd was nearly as big as the last time and the Wise One was talking to the same man as when she'd first seen him. The man was thanking the Wise One. It seemed that his female relatives had, miraculously, responded to his suggestion and were at home working contentedly with their wool and contributing to household expenses.

The Wise One said he was most gratified to hear that.

Someone had left him a basket of bread and meat, which he had by his side. He snuck a bite from time to time, and he patted his rather abundant belly. Lately, he had been watching his weight, eating only when he was hungry and drinking only when he was thirsty. Still, he said sadly, his stomach continued to grow. He then spoke of dancing exercises, which he did every evening to keep the situation from getting any more out of hand. Someone in the crowd asked for a demonstration. He got up and gave a brief but spirited performance, which delighted the crowd.

Another man, obviously not one of the Wise One's admirers, began heckling him. Pandora was amazed at how unruffled Socrates remained. "Why don't you teach your wife some manners?" the man cried out. The Wise One laughed; obviously this wasn't the first time he had heard this. He said that his great aim in life was to get on well with people and he chose his wife because he knew that if he could get along with her, he could get along with anyone.

It was only then that he saw Pandora, walking around the edge of the crowd. He nudged Phoenix, who had been standing next to him this whole time, as if to give him permission to go and see her. Phoenix had seen Pandora the moment she came over the crest.

Pandora got right to the point. How had she gotten home? For the past week she had been going over it again and again. She remembered saying good-bye to the Wise One and thanking him most profusely, thanks to the wine. She remembered him patting her on the head and saying to Phoenix, "Take care, my boy, you are transporting precious cargo."

But that was it. The next thing she remembered was waking up just before daybreak in her own bed. How did she get from the party to her house? And, even more mysteriously, up to her room and into her nightdress?

Pandora didn't like things like this. She didn't like not being in control of herself and not remembering things.

At first, Phoenix laughed at the intensity of her concern. He tried to brush aside her questions, but Pandora was insistent. Seeing that he had no choice and that she took the matter much more seriously than he did, he calmly told her what had happened.

He had borrowed a cart from their host, and they

rode in that back to her house. Pandora was upset that she had absolutely no memory of this. She urged Phoenix to be as specific and descriptive as possible, hoping that that would make the memory return.

She sat next to him, and they talked the whole way, or almost the whole way. Pandora pressed him, wanting to know about what, specifically.

About him and when his father had been ostracized by the Assembly and exiled. And how Phoenix returned to Athens alone and met the Wise One, who was a friend of his father's.

They talked about the Wise One, his teachings, and what it was like to be with him all day.

And they talked about the party and whether or not anyone suspected that she was really a girl. And how worried she was about that even though he assured her most of the guests were either too concerned with themselves or had drunk too much wine to be suspicious of much of anything.

Did they talk the whole way? Pandora wanted to know. There was something he wasn't saying, she could tell. Intuition. Not something he was lying about, just something he was holding back.

"Most of the way," he said. She did lie down, briefly, to take a nap. She hoped he would go on, but he didn't. How on earth had she gotten to her room? she asked.

The journey had taken much longer than he thought it would because they took the long way to avoid the rocks and inclines and also because of the headstrong nature of the donkey. Pandora was fast asleep by the time they reached her house. No matter how hard Phoenix shook her, she only moaned, "Go away," and rolled over. He didn't know what to do and simply sat there on the back of the cart, thinking over the impossible nature of his situation.

Just then, someone came out of the house. He was petrified but he didn't want to run or hide or act like they had done anything wrong, which they hadn't or mostly hadn't, he said, hoping Pandora would know what he meant, which she did.

It was a woman, and she said that she was Pandora's stepmother. She was most concerned that her stepdaughter was unharmed. Once Phoenix assured her most emphatically that she wasn't harmed in any way and was just sleeping rather soundly, Charis explained that she had heard her stepdaughter leave and had been waiting for her return.

Then they, the two of them, carried Pandora up to her room.

Needless to say Pandora was shocked by this revelation. Her stepmother had known! Had heard her leaving! Why didn't she stop her? Why didn't she say anything in the morning? And why didn't she say anything, even now?

Worse Than That

Pandora thanked the gods that the next week flew by. By the time she got to the Fountain House, her head was filled with questions she hoped the Wise One would address. Her heart was pounding in anticipation of seeing Phoenix again.

As soon as she arrived she knew something was the matter. Phoenix was there but looked extremely distressed. The Wise One was nowhere to be seen. All the girls were huddled behind the Fountain House, whispering to one another conspiratorially and looking at her. Her first thought was that the Wise One had died. In a way the news was worse than that.

She had never seen Phoenix look so grave. Usually he had such a carefree countenance, even after he fainted that first day. That was why she thought he was so much younger than he really was. Now he looked all of his seventeen years.

He took her by the arm and led her away from the Fountain House.

The Wise One had been arrested!

Pandora felt like someone had struck her. Her head was immediately filled with urgent questions: by whom, for what, where was he, was he all right, would he be all right?

Phoenix waited for her to calm down and began to explain.

The official indictment charged Socrates with corrupting the morals of the young people of Athens. It said that he refused to recognize the gods sanctioned by the state. That he was teaching the young people to discard conventional gods and worship the new deities he was teaching them about.

That was only the official indictment. There were more dire things at work behind the scenes.

Powerful people both in and out of the government were tired of the way he was constantly exposing them — constantly pointing his finger and sticking his nose where it didn't belong. They were tired of his making fools of them in public. Tired of his laughing at them and giving other people reason to laugh at them.

And there was more. More that wasn't contained in the official documents. He was suspected and being accused, unofficially, of a whole host of crimes.

They claimed Socrates taught the children of Athens to treat their fathers with contempt, by convincing them that they knew what was best for themselves and that they were smarter than their fathers.

They had witnesses who had heard him advocating confining certifiably insane fathers, and that it was justified because the ignorant should always be kept under restraint by the wise.

They were demanding the death penalty, Phoenix said, so softly she could hardly hear him.

Pandora had heard enough: She wanted to attend the trial. Phoenix said that would be impossible, but he could see from the look in Pandora's eyes that it *was* possible. That he was going to make it possible.

She dismissed his concern that she would get caught leaving the house. That was her problem; he should just worry about getting her into the courthouse.

Seeing he had no choice, Phoenix said he would take care of everything.

Bridge the Abyss

Bridge the Abyss

⚘   ⚘   ⚘

When Pandora returned home, her father and brother were in the midst of an animated discussion about the Wise One's arrest. They were so engrossed that they didn't even hear her come in, which was all the better as far as she was concerned.

According to Alcander, all of Athens was talking about the arrest. Everyone he spoke to at the agora said that Socrates would flee the country. Her father agreed. "He'll never stand trial," he said. "He's got the word out already. He has friends with lots and lots of money, and they are already planning his escape."

Pandora didn't know what to think. Part of her was overjoyed to hear that the Wise One was going to escape. But she didn't trust what her father said.

He liked to sound as if he had inside information and just couldn't reveal his sources. But as she got older, Pandora had realized that most of the time he was wrong. He talked like he knew, but he didn't.

"The government will be happy to get rid of him without a long, controversial trial," Alcander said.

Polybius said that his teacher Lysias thought that Socrates would not respond seriously to the charges. That he would refuse to give them that kind of recognition. Lysias said Socrates's followers were going to speak at the trial in his defense.

When Pandora got upstairs to her room, she was startled to find her stepmother sitting on the bed, waiting for her. It looked as if she had been sitting there for a long time.

Pandora pretended to look out the window. She had already seen the look on her stepmother's face, and she didn't want to see it again.

The whole world was in that look.

It was a world of misunderstanding and distance. Of not wanting it to be that way but being unable to do anything about it. It was a look of trying. Of believing that trying counted for something. That trying could narrow the breach and lessen the wound.

But trying couldn't bridge the abyss.

Pandora knew in her heart that her stepmother deserved something. She didn't deserve just to be shut out. Pandora hadn't forgotten the love her stepmother had so willingly provided after her mother died, when Pandora was drowning in a sea of uncertainty and unfathomable loss. She hadn't forgotten the love she had given her at a time when she was so desperate she didn't even know she needed it.

She considered telling her the truth but wasn't sure she knew it herself. Talking to her stepmother would be futile anyway — they lived in separate worlds. And, besides, the truth she did know she couldn't risk telling her. Because the truth was, she didn't care about a dowry or a wedding or having nuts and sweets sprinkled over her head. And she didn't care about Meander and never would. She didn't want to disappoint her uncle or cause her stepmother any pain, but she had known from the moment she first saw Phoenix that he was the boy she would marry.

Her stepmother had always listened to her, and now she appeared to be listening even harder, as if she knew how important it was — even though Pandora hadn't uttered a single word.

"Each generation," Charis began, tears welling up in her eyes, "thinks differently than the one before. Sometimes the difference is great and sometimes it is small, but always it is there, and always it separates them."

Speaking From the Heart

The five hundred jurors chosen for the trial sat on wooden benches and listened as the prosecution presented its case, essentially restating the indictment.

The prosecutors stood on an elevated platform that looked like a stage to Pandora. How ironic, she thought, that this should be, in a way, the first play she ever attended. She wished it were a comedy and not the tragedy that it was.

When they were finished the Wise One spoke.

To Pandora, sitting next to Phoenix in the spectators' seats, it was clear that Socrates had not formally prepared a speech in his own defense. And it was also clear to the two of them, as it was to all of those there who knew the Wise One, that he was speaking from the heart.

The eloquence was conveyed not by the style and delivery but because of the artless, unaffected sincerity of the words themselves.

First, he apologized to the jury for being unfamiliar with the appropriate way of speaking in a courtroom. He had never, in his seventy years on earth, been in a courtroom, so he asked them to please excuse his conversational manner.

Listening to his accusers had almost made him forget who he was. He assured the jury that there was no truth in what they were saying.

There were, however, things he *was* willing to admit to.

He did urge people to be individuals and to follow their own paths, to "know thyself," as the oracle said.

If he were being accused of being concerned that his fellow citizens were, more and more with each passing day, neglecting what was of real importance and spending their lives on trivialities, then he pleaded guilty to that as well.

If he were being accused of questioning many of

those who called themselves wise but were not, then he pleaded guilty to that. It bothered him greatly that acquiring as much money as possible, as fast as possible, by any means possible, had been recently elevated to a high art, while no time was spent in pursuit of wisdom, truth, and enlightenment. Lately, he warned, the people of Athens seemed to have turned their attention to greed rather than good.

Wealth does not bring goodness, but goodness brings wealth, he added.

The jury, after retiring to vote by secret ballot, returned to deliver the verdict. The vote was close but Socrates was found guilty.

Now the Wise One had the opportunity to offer an alternative to the death penalty.

He had appeared unfazed by the verdict and un-afraid of the sentence. The door had been opened, and he was prepared to walk through it.

"What penalty do I deserve to suffer in view of what I myself think that I have done?" he asked.

He had not led a conventional life. Never cared about the things that other people cared about: money, possessions, a big house, a prestigious job.

Long ago, he had decided to go down the road less traveled. To devote his life to convincing those who chose to listen to him to abandon concerns for practical things and concern themselves with the conditions of their souls.

He could never stop being a philosopher. If he had to live his life the way the government wanted and not the way he thought best, then he would prefer death.

The important thing is not to live but to live well.

He paused before specifically answering the question posed: an alternate punishment.

What he truly deserved in return for what he had done was to be given free dining in the finest restaurants in Athens for the rest of his life.

⚓

He had spoken for three hours.

The juror who controlled the water clock noted that the entire trial had taken nine and a half hours.

Maintain Her Balance

It seemed as if the first thirteen years of Pandora's life were lived at one speed and that now everything was happening a hundred times faster. Even the most ordinary things — getting up in the morning, eating, doing the chores — were merely blurs, streaming before her eyes.

Even more unsettling was the speed with which the many extraordinary things were happening: meeting the Wise One, hearing about her engagement to Meander, cutting her hair, going to the party, Phoenix, and now this — the Wise One's trial and conviction.

It was simply impossible to absorb it all. It was all Pandora could do just to maintain her balance.

Waiting for Phoenix at the bottom of the hill, she wished she could have been with him, at the Wise One's side. The idea of Socrates being put in jail at his age was too horrible for Pandora to consider for very long.

When Phoenix arrived, hours late, she could see, even in the darkness of the waning half-moon night, that the news was not good. She urged him to tell her everything.

The Wise One had been surrounded by his friends the entire time, although it hardly seemed necessary. His bearing was sublime. They tried to convince him to escape, besieging him with arguments: his obligation to his family, not allowing his enemies to win out, not allowing people to blame them for not saving him.

More than enough money, they explained, had been raised in anticipation. Not only that, a number of destinations had assured them that he would be most welcomed.

It did no good; he refused to run away.

The only thing he complained about was that his legs were hurting from the chains. He sat up in bed and insisted that they talk about the things they always had. Things that were important: why the unexamined life is not worth living and about the immortality of the soul.

Meanwhile, the executioner mixed the hemlock. He advised the Wise One to talk as little as possible because that might affect the action of the poison, perhaps making a second and third dose necessary.

That's when he waved away the others and signaled Phoenix to come closer. He said that he had a message of the utmost importance for him to give Pandora.

"Ask her," he said, "if she remembers when we first met. If she remembers the story I told her of the origins of her name. We were interrupted, and I had to rush off before the story was finished. The story of her name.

"Tell her that, as frightened as she was, Pandora — the original Pandora — still had the presence of mind to put the lid back on the opening in time to save the one good thing that remained in the jar that hadn't escaped. Hope. Hope remained at the bottom of the vessel and hope will always remain. Whatever evil surrounds us, hope never entirely leaves us. Tell her she must always remember that."

Then the Wise One gathered everyone around,

emptied the cup of hemlock, and lay back down in the bed. After a while, he said he was losing feeling in his feet and he could feel his legs grow stiff, cold, and heavy.

They knew that when the stiffness reached his heart, it would be over.

"Well, now," he said, "it is time to be off. I to die and you to live; but which of us has the happier prospect is unknown to anyone but the gods."

❧

Then there was only silence between Pandora and Phoenix. Not the silence that occurs hundreds, maybe thousands of times each day, but an ominous silence. The kind of silence that signifies that whatever follows, your life will never be the same.

"I must leave," Phoenix said. "Leave Athens. I can no longer live here after what has happened. One of my father's ships is set to sail at dawn. I know the captain well, and there will be no problem, but we must go now. . . ."

We? thought Pandora.

"We must go now and hide down at the harbor and wait for daybreak. We can't risk your returning to the house. It is too risky — someone might see you and try to stop you. There is too much to lose, I can't contemplate being without you. Please say yes."

Which Pandora did, taking his hand without speaking a word.

Historical Note

Almost every facet of our lives today — from politics to art, from cities to sports — was developed by the ancient Greeks. Over a period of approximately 3,000 years, the ancient Greeks created one of the world's most important and innovative civilizations, which continues to fascinate and inspire us today.

Many of the early communities of Greece settled along the coasts or on the islands surrounding the mainland and, therefore, depended heavily on the Aegean Sea for trade and supplies. Hence, the Greeks became skilled sailors and were able to visit the people of different cultures, learn their customs, and enjoy their goods. Most Greek settlements gradually transformed themselves into independent city-states, with somewhere between 1,000 and 5,000 people living in each one. In the early days of Greece, the city-states, or *poleis*, as they were called, were governed by their own kings, many of whom were ruthless tyrants. Uprisings, violence, and wars were common at the time.

By 800 B.C., the Greek city-states, defending themselves against invaders, began to develop a different system of government in which a group of rulers replaced the king: an oligarchy. As a result of better management, the city-states became wealthier and more powerful. The two main city-states were Athens, a hub of commerce and culture, and Sparta, a militaristic society that isolated itself from outside influence. With stability came a period of unprecedented advancement.

At this time, artwork became more complex and precise. Early poets such as Homer and Hesiod wrote epic poems about the heroes and the gods, and in 776 B.C., the first Olympic games were held. In 585 B.C., in the city-state of Miletus, a few wise men congregated to discuss the nature of the world around them. What, they wondered, was the world made of? Some, observing melting ice, said the world was made out of water; others, looking at boiling water turn into steam, said the world was made out of air. Together, these men — Thales, Anaximander, Heraclitus, and Pythagoras — created a new science: philosophy.

The ancient Greeks examined not only the nature of the physical world, but also the nature of man himself and of the best possible society men could hope for. Slowly, oligarchy made way for a new concept, democracy, which comes from the Greek word *demos,* meaning people. Democracy allowed a greater number of citizens to participate in deciding on how to run the *polis.* Greek democracies, however, were nothing like democratic governments we know today; only the free, male citizens of the city-states were allowed to participate, while women, slaves, and foreigners were excluded.

The Greek city-states continued to flourish, developing drama, sculpture, and geometry, as well as their religion — which we know today mainly through the intricate mythology of gods and goddesses. In 490 B.C., however, the Greek civilization faced a major danger. Persia, the greatest military empire in western Asia, conquered several Greek cities, and then moved to destroy Athens with an army of 150,000 men and 600 ships. The Athenians, joined by citizens of other Greek city-states, chiefly Corinth and Sparta, fought a series of naval battles for eleven bloody years, until they finally defeated the Persians.

Now the major force in Greece, Athens used the vast navy it had built to fight the Persians and turned itself into an empire of trade, wealth, and culture. Other city-states, however, were not pleased with Athens's rise to power. In 431 B.C., the Spartans, whose powerful army outnumbered the Athenians two to one, invaded Athenian land, burning crops in an attempt to starve the Athenian people and force them to surrender. The Peloponnesian War went on for nearly thirty years and spread to the furthest corners of Greece. It was, by far, the most deadly battle the world had ever known. Thousands of men died and countless others were wiped away by plagues and famine.

The Athenians tried their best but proved unsuccessful against Sparta's militaristic genius. In 405 B.C., the last of the once-mighty Athenian fleet was destroyed, and Athens was stripped of its wealth.

The Spartan conquerors set up a new government in Athens, an oligarchy composed of thirty nobles, known as the Thirty Tyrants. The Tyrants ruled Athens with great cruelty and brutality. Under their reign, only a few Athenians enjoyed citizen rights, and the rest could be imprisoned or killed without the privilege of standing trial. Some of Athens's heroes were exiled or managed to escape and, aided by other city-states that feared Sparta's might, returned to Athens two years later to overthrow the Tyrants and restore democracy.

During this time of great political turmoil, a philosopher named Socrates had become increasingly popular among the young nobles of Athens. Thoughtful and observant, Socrates baffled Athens's youth not by professing wisdom but by claiming ignorance. "I only know," he would famously say, "that I know nothing." Instead of simply giving lectures, as most teachers did at the time, Socrates favored asking his pupils questions, engaging young men in dialogue, and helping them form opinions about important topics such as love, virtue, wisdom, and justice.

Gradually, Socrates became more and more of a

celebrity, but the government began to think he was corrupting the minds of the city's youth. In 399 B.C., Socrates was brought to trial, under two charges: corrupting young people and interfering with Athenian religion. Tried before a jury of his peers, as well as before a large crowd of spectators, Socrates delivered a speech in his own defense, which his student Plato recorded in a book known as *The Apology*. In his typical style, Socrates did not simply deny the charges against him but instead used the trial as yet another opportunity for raising questions about morality, virtue, and duty. He was found guilty and sentenced to death.

Socrates was offered banishment, but ever the Athenian patriot, he refused. After the trial, some of Socrates's followers tried to convince him that he should flee the city to escape his looming execution; still, he refused. All his life, he said, he had preached the importance of obeying laws, and now when his time had come to obey the law, he had no other option. A sympathetic guard slipped Socrates a cupful of poison, and surrounded by his weeping pupils, he took his own life.

Even after Socrates's death, the study of philosophy, science, and art continued, as did the occasional battle. By approximately 200 B.C., however, Greece was no longer the greatest empire in the world; it had been replaced by the republic of Rome. In 130 B.C., Rome conquered Greece, adopting a great deal of its culture along the way. The golden age of Greek civilization had ended, but its immense contributions to the way human beings understand themselves, one another, and the world around them remain today.

- In 525 B.C., the first theatrical plays, which grew out of festivals honoring the god Dionysus, were written and performed. Aeschylus is considered to be the first playwright who began the important tradition of tragic drama.
- Archimedes, a Greek mathematician, discovered the Principle of Floating Bodies while taking a bath. He noticed that the more he inserted his body into the water, the more water overflowed from the tub. He ran outside into the street, screaming "*Eureka!*" which is Greek for "I have found it!" People, however, did not bathe on a daily basis until the time of the Roman Empire.

- The Greeks were the first to regularly cut their hair, thereby inventing barbershops. The barbershop was a place for Greek men to meet and talk about politics, sports, and gossip.
- More than 40,000 men came to watch the first Olympic Games in 776 B.C. The only event in the games was a 200-yard race. Through the years, other events, such as boxing, discus throwing, wrestling, and chariot races were added as well. The tradition was revived in 1896 by a French baron wishing to promote world peace. The first modern Olympic Games were held in Athens.

ABOUT THE AUTHOR

Barry Denenberg is the highly acclaimed author of many books for young readers, including, *Voices from Vietnam*, which was praised by *Booklist* in a starred review for being a "high-caliber oral history expressly for young adults." He is also the author of *An American Hero: The True Story of Charles A. Lindbergh*; *Nelson Mandela: No Easy Walk to Freedom*; *Stealing Home: The Story of Jackie Robinson*; and *All Shook Up: The Life and Death of Elvis Presley*, all of which received extraordinary reviews. Mr. Denenberg is also the author of *Atticus of Rome*, another book in the Life and Times series.

Mr. Denenberg has written several books for the Dear America line, including *Early Sunday Morning*; *One Eye Laughing, The Other Weeping*; *When Will this Cruel War Be Over?*; *So Far from Home*; and *Mirror, Mirror on the Wall*; and for My Name Is America, *The Journal of Ben Uchida* and *The Journal of William Thomas Emerson*.

An excerpt from . . .

THE LIFE AND TIMES

ATTICUS OF ROME
30 B.C.

BY BARRY DENENBERG

A SMELL DARKER
AND MORE THREATENING
THAN ANIMAL TERROR

❖ ◆ ❖ ◆ ❖

Last night, Atticus had had the dream again.

At the beginning of the dream, the sky was clear blue and the midday sun was unbearably hot. But now, later in the dream, it was dusk, and Atticus could feel the darkness approaching. The air was thick with a yellow haze that nearly enveloped him and blocked out the rays of the sun, making the heat less oppressive.

He was standing naked and alone in the middle of a vast arena — at least he thought it was an arena. He couldn't see well enough to tell for sure. But he sensed that something was out there, just beyond the yellow haze. People, hundreds, maybe thousands. He could feel their presence.

Periodically the haze would thin. Then he would see, or think he saw, waving white handkerchiefs. He wondered if they were waving at him and, if they were, why. Were they trying to warn him of something? And if so, what?

There was a sound in the distance. Loud enough to distinguish it from silence but too far away for him to identify its nature. Sometimes, when the wind shifted, the sound became more distinct. It wasn't one sound, it was many sounds. The clash of steel on steel. A trumpet announcing he didn't know what. And there was more, even fainter, but still there. He could hear it if he stood perfectly still: wild animals, roaring mightily, somewhere in the haze.

The sounds frightened Atticus. He wanted to clasp his hands hard over his ears, shutting them out and putting an end to the frightening feeling. He hesitated, afraid to make a sudden move.

There were smells, too. The air was rancid and yet perfumed. He could smell the animals. He could smell their terror. He had smelled it before, hunting with his father. But this was different. This was the smell of animals that were trapped, caged, pacing, near panic.

There was another, even more terrifying smell fouling the air. A smell he had never encountered. A smell darker and more threatening than animal terror.

Were his ears playing tricks on him? At times the animals seemed to be out there, in the distance. At other times he thought he could hear them and feel them beneath him, underground, just below his feet. He could feel the earth shaking and rumbling, as if it were about to heave up and split, revealing an abyss into which he would fall and be lost forever.

LIKE THE GODS
ANNOUNCING THE END
OF TIME

❖ ◆ ❖ ◆ ❖

It was always at this point, never before and never after, that Atticus would awake, drenched in a cold sweat. It took him a while to realize where he was and even longer to remember how he came to be there.

Images flashed inside his head, appearing and evaporating:

His village, peaceful in the early morning hours.

His neighbors, like Atticus and his family, either half asleep or just beginning to stir about.

There had been no warning that day.

The Roman soldiers had vanquished the sentries guarding the village and easily overcome the fortifications that had taken so long to construct. Fortifications in which the villagers had fruitlessly put their faith.

Now there was no time. No time to think. No time to act.

The cavalry was already upon them, riding at full gallop, their swords drawn from their scabbards and glistening in the first rays of dawn, their horses' hooves pounding the ground like the gods announcing the end of time.

The infantry, wave upon wave of them: more than the grass that covered the ground or the sand on the beach. More men than Atticus had ever seen in his life converged on their defenseless town. Hundreds, maybe thousands, it was impossible to say. They were everywhere at once, impervious, protected by their huge shields and brass helmets. Slaughtering the frantic villagers while they slept or made futile attempts at escape.

And there was no time to say good-bye.

Before he knew it his father had pulled him from their hut, which had been struck by one of the flaming arrows, launched by unseen archers, falling on the village like a hailstorm from hell. But his mother and sister were still in there, trapped, their screams muffled by the crackling of the flames.

There was no time for comprehension, no time for grieving. Only moments later he and his father, along with a handful of other survivors, were being shackled, chained and dragged into captivity, their lives shattered and lost.

Three days later Atticus was separated from his father and sold to a slave trader. Tears flowed now, blurring his vision as he struggled to retain one last image of his beloved father, forced to stand powerless and mute as his son was taken from him.